JACK & the Sly Fox

A Tale About Discovering Your Treasures Within

Illustrations by
IVAN NATARENG MARTINEZ

Written by
WES HALL

**Attention Corporations, Universities, Colleges
and Nonprofit Organizations:**

Quantity discounts are available on bulk purchases of this book for educational or gift purposes or as a premium for increasing magazine subscriptions and renewals. Special books or book excerpts also can be created to fit specific needs. For information, please contact the author or visit the Web site at www.totallymotivatedpress.com.

For information, contact:

Totally Motivated Inc.
2204 W. 42nd Street
Los Angeles, CA 90008
213-973-8203

Printed in the United States of America

Illustrations by Ivan Natareng Martinez

Cover design and page layout by MagicGraphix.com

ISBN 978-0-615-90761-1

This book is dedicated to
you rare souls who beat the odds,
found your gifts, and used them to
make the world a better place for us all.

Acknowledgements:

You can't accomplish great things without great people, and I want to thank the great people who helped make this project a reality. I must first thank my Lord and Savior Jesus Christ for leading me to this message and allowing me to be the vessel through which it is delivered to the world.

Brenda Manuel

Cara Riggs

Richard Galbreath

Larry Parker

Cheries Dupee

Ebony Hawkins

Curtis Conyears

Janette Conyears – Auguar

Karen Davis

Kimberly Nash

Madeline Churchich

Gary Peters

Thank you so much for your generous contribution!
Wes

Table of
Contents

JACK
& the
Sly Fox

JACK

GEORGE
THE SLY FOX

A Tale about Discovering
Your Treasures Within

"Do not chase after money; instead, discover your
own inner-power, for it is that inner-power that will
attract to you, your greatest reward."
—We Shall217

JACK AND THE SLY FOX

On the planet Shurefire, lived King Zerias, the most powerful King in the galaxy. His massive army comprised of the deadliest soldiers, struck fear into any, who would consider attacking his kingdom.

The King's power was so great that no one dared speak ill of him, for it was known from the cluster planets of Galmastes to the remote regions of Iptor that he possessed the gift of clairvoyance and could hear the thoughts of others. Countless stories were told of what happened to those who unwisely crossed the King.

The King's heart, however, had one soft spot – his young son, Jack. While others dared not challenge the King, young Jack possessed no such fear. Jack's rebellion against his father grew with each passing day. His young eyes saw his father's power and wanted that power for himself. One day in a fit of rage Jack spoke the unthinkable, "I hope you die soon, so I can be King!"

The King was very hurt and disappointed. That night he tossed and turned in his bed, desperately wondering what to do with his beloved, yet rebellious son. The next morning he arrived at a decision. "I will call upon my faithful and all-seeing servants, "The Powerful Ones," they will provide me with an answer," thought the King. With one single thought he reached across the galaxy and summoned The Powerful Ones to come before him.

Authurius, Uthor and Dominacus, were the mystical servants of the kings. They were known throughout the land as the "Powerful Ones." They came from the dead-sun planet known as Getharr and were ageless. They stayed to themselves and were rumored to have god-like powers.

The beauty of a clear sunshiny day was briefly disrupted by the ear-deafening sound of a gigantic lightning bolt. The bolt of lightning struck with such force it split the ground and dust flew high into the sky. When the dust cleared The Powerful Ones appeared. With a movement of their hands the ground came together and they continued on to find the King.

The graceful movement of The Powerful Ones was always a curiosity to those who came into contact with them because; no one had actually seen their feet. It appeared as if they floated more than walked and the bottom of their pure white garments never dirtied.

King Zerias saw his faithful servants approaching and waved them to his side. The Powerful Ones bowed before the King and sent messages of love and adoration to him. The King touched the shoulder of each of his servants and bid them to rise. "We have much to discuss," said the King.

The Powerful Ones listened to the King and his problem. They could tell the King was distressed and really desired their help. "Give us three days, wise King, and we will provide you an answer to your problem," said Authurius.

The Powerful Ones

The Powerful Ones in all their wisdom knew well the importance of the task before them. The King loved his son and would not take kindly to him being hurt. Although the King respected their gifts and position he would call for their destruction if they mishandled such a delicate assignment as this. The first night each man sat in silence thinking alone about how to best deal with young Jack.

After many hours of silence, Authurius spoke, "It is hard to see the light of a candle when it's next to the sun."

"Young legs never grow strong when someone else is doing the carrying," said Uthor. "A boy will never learn to create on his own, if all the creating has been done for him," Dominacus said. That was day one.

On the second day, The Powerful Ones joined together and began putting together the plan for young Jack. "The boy must learn how to fend for himself," said Authurius. "We must find a way to place all the powers he needs inside him," beamed Uthor.

"A look of concern crossed Dominacus' face. We must do something his father will not like," he said.

The two Powerful Ones looked at their friend and examined his thoughts.

The three had performed many great tasks together and their thoughts were as one but this time Dominacus' thoughts seemed strange and far away from the other two.

"We must send the boy to another place," said Dominacus.

"Why must this be done?" asked Uthor.

"Only alone can he learn to be responsible for his decisions. When he is by himself he will be forced to create his own way. When times get hard he will have to find a way to overcome difficulties, on his own," Dominacus said.

Uthor and Authurius knew Dominacus was right. They also knew the King would not look kindly upon this decision. "This matter must be handled with extreme care, lest the King call for our heads," Authurius said. That was day two.

In the morning of the third day, The Powerful Ones arose. Each knew the other's thoughts. They had worked together for many lifetimes and understood the inner workings of the universe. Each wore many seals of battle, branded into his skin, including the most honored seal of Atar, only granted to a War-king who has slain a Dark-Dragon with his bare hands.

"We must place special powers inside young Jack that will serve him and make him into a great and wise ruler! We must give him an identity that sets him apart from every other human on the planet. He must know he is special, one of a kind, and able to do all things he sets out to accomplish," said Dominacus.

The Powerful Ones sat in a circle, each with his legs folded into a triangle. They communicated with one another without saying a word. Each had been given the power to create gifts and talents. With a great force they joined their minds together and began to create the gifts, and talents to be placed inside Jack.

A special candle placed in the corner of the room was the only source of light. A soft wind began to blow through the window of the hut. At first, a light rustling of wind could be heard in the room and then the rustling turned into a mighty wind.

The mighty wind was alive and although its force was strong, it did not disturb the thoughts of The Powerful Ones. One by one, gifts began to appear. The gifts were made of a special energy. The energy was made from the universe itself. Each gift was from an ancient time, yet new, unique, and alive.

Suddenly the wind stopped and the room was eerily silent. The Powerful Ones opened their eyes and beheld the new gifts and talents that would be placed inside Jack. Each gift floated in mid-air. Each piece of energy made a soft humming noise and appeared to have its own special pulse.

THE GIFTS

$\mathcal{B}$ right colors filled the room as each gift radiated its own special light. The Powerful Ones stood and looked at each gift. They were pleased with their creations and knew they would serve Jack well. These gifts were the most potent gifts in the universe; special powers for a special child.

Authurius stood next to the gift that shined the brightest. Its glow was orange and red on the inside and bright white and blue on its outer area. It had strange lines drawn on its surface and it vibrated greater than the others.

"This gift will be called Odonus (meaning Individual Sign). Odonus will be placed in Jack's hand, and no one else on the planet will have this print. If he ever needs proof of how special he is all he has to do is rub his fingers and the proof will be his. This special power will make his voice different from anyone else on the planet, too, and when he speaks his voice will be great, and commanding," said Authurius.

"Jack is the son of a King and this special code in his hand will represent the mark of the King. His new world will call it a fingerprint. Although all on the planet possess a unique fingerprint, Jack's will be more unique than all," Authurius said.

Uthor rose and stood by a gift. The gift appeared to dance as he grew near. The gift was the color of the galaxy and sparkled like radiant diamonds. Its energy began to change from solid to wind, and inside its shape new worlds could be seen forming.

"This gift will be called Arius (meaning the Creator's Pulse). Arius will be placed in young Jack's heart. The energy of Arius can make something out of nothing. By using this gift, Jack's ability to create will be unlimited. He will be able to use the ground to make clay, the clay to make bricks, and the bricks to make huge buildings," said Uthor.

"With Arius, Jack can become the ruler of his world and attract the greatest amounts of wealth. With the power of Arius in his heart all he has to do is desire a new life, believe it can be done, and move toward it. The energy of Arius will do the rest ... if only he believes." Uthor continued.

Electricity flowed through the hands of The Powerful Ones as they shaped and molded pure universal energy. That same power was to be given to young Jack and the power to create anything his mind could imagine would be his.

Dominacus stood and examined the next gift. The gift looked like the number eight lying on its side. The gift made a humming noise as its vibration moved in a circle. Inside the gift were amazing new inventions, inventions that would change the world.

"This gift will be called Farlight – "Farlight" (meaning The Vision). We will place Farlight in Jack's mind and it will show him great things that are yet to come. Farlight will speak to him while he walks and show him great things in his dreams. All he has to do is believe in the things Farlight shows him and he will bring forth great inventions that will make him wealthy ... if only he believes," said Dominacus.

"Farlight is the creator of the imagination. The gift sees into the future and shows great things to come. Things vibrate faster in the imagination realm, than things in the physical world. Jack will have to learn to focus and slow the vibrations down if he is to use them in his new life," Dominacus said.

Dominacus, Uthor and Authurius continued examining and naming each of the six gifts. "These six gifts will aid Jack greatly!" said Uthor. They were satisfied with their creations and happy young Jack would have what he needed to be successful – if only he believes. They gathered the special gifts and headed off to present them to the King.

Chapter Three

THE ANSWER

"Wise King," Authurius began, "we have returned and with us, the solution to your problem." The King studied the faces of his faithful servants anxiously waiting for what they had to say. "Come, tell me what you have determined," said the King.

The Powerful Ones followed the King into his massive palace. The imperial guards of the palace stepped aside, bowing slightly to the King as he entered. Statues of Knights on horses, winged angels, and golden ornaments filled the room. This was a room of great grandeur. A room fit for a King. He motioned for The Powerful Ones to be seated.

At the King's beckoning, Authurius spoke. "We have created a potion that will cause young Jack to forget who he is," said Authurius. The King was confused. "Why would I want to do such a thing" he asked sternly?

Slowly and carefully, The Powerful Ones shared their plan with the King. "The boy thinks he knows what it is to be King. He thinks your job is easy. His questioning has turned into disrespect. The boy must be sent away for a time to a strange land, and forget he is the son of a King." The Powerful Ones spoke to the King without using their voices. They spoke to his heart and mind adding the energy of love to their words to help the King receive the message.

The King began to understand but his love for his son made it difficult to fathom sending him somewhere he could be harmed. "How will he eat and how will he take care of himself?" the King asked. "We will hide special powers inside of him. Anyone who comes in contact with the boy will recognize his power. The special powers once developed will attract the attention of great men and they will give him all the money he needs to live an abundant life," said Uthor.

Although he wished there was a better way, the King understood. The Powerful Ones would place special gifts and talents inside his son that will make him a mighty creative force. His very vibration will attract the people and opportunities he needs to enable him to live a life of abundance. The boy's job will be to discover his special gifts and bring them out. The gifts and talents will do the rest. Still the King was troubled.

"What will happen if he doesn't work to bring out his special gifts?" asked the King. The Powerful Ones looked to one another before one spoke. They were fearful of telling the King the truth, but knew he must be told. "If the boy does not work hard to discover and develop his gifts he will live the life of a beggar," said Dominacus.

The King stood up, his brow wrinkled into a frown, his eyes became icy black and he stared into the souls of The Powerful Ones. Dominacus, Uthor and Authurius could feel the anger of the King, and knew they must speak swiftly to help the King understand.

"To be King of the Universe you had to endure great trials, your Highness," Said Authurius. The Powerful Ones reminded the King how he himself had to work hard to become King. Becoming the king required great strength and great courage. They reminded him of the countless battles he had fought and the time he single-handedly fought with Tyress the Man-Beast on the planet Fandor, a battle that lasted 47 days. The King's anger subsided as he listened to his wise servants. With a heavy sigh the King exhaustedly slumped back down into his chair. He knew they spoke the truth, to be King one must go through great trials, and endure great hardships.

"Mighty King," said Authurius, please allow us to show you the gifts we have created for young Jack. We have searched the galaxies to secure the mystical secrets and energy that will transform him from a boy-child into a great king."

"Show me," said the King!

THE KING

The King examined each gift closely. Each gift appeared to recognize the King's energy and responded to his kingly touch. A smile appeared on his face as he examined the Gift of Creation. "You have done well; my faithful servants and you shall each receive a great reward!" As quickly as he spoke, his ruffled brow gave way to another thought. "Wait, there is one more gift my son must have," said the King!

A look of confusion covered the faces of The Powerful Ones. "Wise King, have we failed you" Uthor asked? "We have searched the universe and called upon the greatest seekers to make sure Jack has all he needs to live a great and successful life, yet you say there is more? Tell us, great and powerful King, what gift have we overlooked," Uthor queried.

The King looked into the faces of his servants. He knew they would rather die than disappoint him. They loved and worshiped him, and only wanted what was best for his son. "You could not have known of this gift because only I can give it," said the King. "One day, my grandchildren will look for me and unless I leave them a way to find me they will forever remain lost."

"This special gift no one can give but me," said the King. "This gift will be passed from generation to generation. It will act as a beacon connecting whoever finds it back to me." The Powerful Ones looked confused. "How will you perform such a feat, great and powerful King? Please tell us," said Authurius.

"Come, I will show you," said the King.

Back to the secret hut went the King, followed by The Powerful Ones. "Sit there," said King Zerias, pointing to a section along the North wall of the Hut. "Direct all your power to the winds of peace, love, protection and adoration. Allow no negative thought to be in this place. Guard this moment with all your might and I will show you how I will give the final gift to my son," he said.

The Gift of Love

No fear or threat of any kind entered the room because The Powerful Ones were on guard and had called upon the mightiest guards of the universe to protect the moment. Death-defying warriors appeared in the room, surrounded the King, and aided the Powerful Ones in protecting the moment. The mighty wind returned and inside it ancient voices could be heard speaking with unknown tongues. The room rocked and shook as if it might be torn asunder The Powerful Ones were undaunted and remained steadfastly connected to their assignment.

King Zerias laid still and allowed the trance to overtake him. Before doing so he had summoned the Sun-goddess Kamar to his side. He shared with her his plan of providing his son with the most special gift and charged her with the task of making it so.

With nurse-like care and the precision of a highly trained surgeon, Kamar removed a small essence of energy from the King. King Zerias groaned as a piece of his kingly being parted from him. A clap of thunder sounded throughout the room, shook the Kingdom, and a piercing light grander than the Star of Taboo, surrounded the King.

The energy of the light was glorious and for an instant caused time to stand still. The light merged with the energy that separated from the king, and together formed an image. The King arose, looked upon the image, and was pleased. He then turned and looked upon his wise servants as they were still protecting the moment as he had commanded them.

"It is done," said the King. The Powerful Ones opened their eyes and could not believe what they saw. "Be not afraid. Things are as they should be," said the King. Uthor, still unable to look upon the vision, spoke, "Wise King, your thoughts are greater than our thoughts and your ways greater than our ways. Please help us to understand what you have done."

"Rise to your feet and look upon what is," said the King. To their utter amazement, standing next to the King was a mirror image of the King himself. The image was softer than anything The Powerful Ones had ever witnessed. In an instant each knew what the King had done.

"I have taken a piece of me to be placed inside my son. I will give him the Gift of Love. This gift will be known as, 'The Greatest Gift of All.' Its force will be the greatest force on the planet. To any who find it, it will light up their soul. To any who give it, no force shall defeat it. And when my grandchildren learn it, it will lead them home to me," said the King.

The Powerful Ones bowed to the King. "Great and wise King, your wisdom is greater than ours. We are at your feet.

You are a great and magnificent ruler," said Dominacus.

The King looked lovingly upon his servants, "Now go and perform your work on my son and prepare him for his new life to come," said King Zerias.

Chapter Five

FAREWELL TO JACK

Jack was asleep when the King and The Powerful Ones entered his room. With a casual movement of his hand authurius caused Jack to fall into a deeper sleep. Jack would not awake until they awakened him.

The gifts were with The Powerful Ones. The glow from each gift made strange and colorful images throughout the room. A gentle humming noise could be heard coming from the gifts because they were alive. One by one, each were placed inside Jack.

Each gift found its place and became one with Jack. Each reduced itself in size, as commanded and waited for him to call upon its service. Although each of the gifts contained enormous power, that power could only come forth through the asking of Jack. The Powerful Ones included one final opportunity for Jack to become aware of the presence of his gifts.

Each gift sent tiny messages to Jack, alerting him to their presence. All Jack had to do was pay attention to the tiny messages and the gifts would automatically reveal their secret powers to him.

The final gift was placed inside Jack and The Powerful Ones were pleased. Now Jack had everything he needed to become great and live a prosperous and abundant life. The King was happy, too. His son could be the ruler of his own world. Jack could become the king he always wanted to be – if only he believes.

The King sat in the room and watched Jack as he slept. He had fought in the greatest battles and never flinched or faltered, but in this moment his heart was heavy, and for the first time in his existence he felt helpless. As he watched his son sleep he briefly turned away. No one noticed the single tear that escaped his eye and tumbled down his cheek. He briskly wiped it away as he continued to gaze at his, soon to be, departed son.

He hoped hard, Jack would find his gifts and come home soon, a changed young man. King Zerias stood and kissed his son's forehead, took a final deep loving look at him, and motioned to The Powerful Ones. With a gesture of their hands Jack was gone and his bed empty. "It is done King. The rest is up to Jack and time," said Authurius.

"As it should be," said the King.

Chapter Six

THE GREATEST TRICK

Jack awoke in a strange land. He had no idea where he was. The memory of the King, his Kingdom, and his previous life was gone. He knew his name and that was it. In the distance he saw people working and shopping in a small town. He wandered for a while and then found an open field to sit, and collect his thoughts. It was a warm summer day and the air blew gently across his face. He felt alone, but not empty.

George the Sly Fox

George was a sly and selfish fox who wanted everything for himself. He wore the most expensive clothes and had the best that money could buy. George's family was known throughout the land as greed-mongers. They would gladly make others work for them and pay their workers little to nothing.

One of George's gifts was the ability to see inside of people. George often used his special ability to see a person's gifts and manipulate them to use their hidden talents to make him money. The fact most people never knew they possessed hidden gifts, made George's job of tricking them into chasing money all the more easier.

George felt good about himself and the way he was able to take advantage of people. He called people names, to himself, and laughed at how easily he could get them to work hard, forsake their talents, and make him money.

While walking down the path leading to town, he saw a boy sitting in the grass. George wondered why the boy was sitting alone and walked over to meet him.

"Hi! "My name is George, what's your name?"

"My name is Jack," Jack replied.

The moment Jack spoke, George's eyes grew large.

Jack noticed George's look and asked him what was wrong.

George was a sly fox. He knew if he told Jack about the gifts hidden inside him, Jack would use them to make money for himself.

As George stared at the gifts inside of Jack, George's heart started beating fast inside his chest. Never had he seen such gifts as these. The gifts vibrated with a greater power than George had ever witnessed. "Who is this person?" George thought to himself. It didn't matter who he was or where he came from, George knew he had found the golden goose.

George knew he had to act fast if he was to keep Jack from discovering his hidden gifts. George reached into his pocket and pulled out a large wad of money and dangled it in front of Jack.

"What's that," ask Jack?

"It's called money," George said. "If you want to dress like me and have all the fine things in life, you have to do everything you can to get as much of this as possible," said George.

Jack was excited to learn about money, "How do I get some?" he asked.

"All you have to do is work for me and I will get it for you," George said.

Jack was happy. He had found a friend (so he thought), someone who would look after him, someone who would help him get some of that stuff called money. All he had to do was work for George and he could have all the things George said he should desire.

THE PAPER CHASE

This world was new for Jack, George was right; everybody was in a race to get their hands on some money. Those who had the money owned the finest horses, cattle, clothing and lived in big houses. He also noticed that those who didn't have money were looked down upon and barely had what they needed to survive.

George smiled to himself as he watched Jack chase after money. The fact Jack came from royalty gave him an appreciation of the finer things and made him chase money all the more. George understood the attraction for Jack and used it to his benefit. George constantly put shiny, beautiful objects in front of Jack; close enough for Jack to touch but never enough money for Jack to own.

George's trick to fool Jack into chasing money instead of discovering and using his gifts worked. Jack had completely ignored the special gifts; The Powerful Ones placed inside of him, and was only looking outside of himself for his treasures.

Jack made George richer and richer by working hard as a salesman. Jack dreamed of being rich and living like George so he worked many long hours. But while George got richer, Jack with all his hard work was barely able to make ends meet.

There was but one man in the town who made his way to the top by those means and George constantly used him as an example for Jack. "See old man John, over there," George said to Jack? Jack looked in the direction that George was pointing.

Jack already knew the story George was about to tell him because George had told him the story a thousand times. "John worked hard all his life and look at him now. He has everything a man could hope for," said George. Actually John didn't have nearly as much as George but John did seem to have everything he needed. "Keep working for me and one day you will have everything you need, too," George said.

George was very sly and created ways to give Jack money and take the money back. He charged Jack fees for staying on his land and eating his food. Jack needed transportation so George charged him a fee for using one of his horses. When Jack needed a place to keep his money, George charged him another fee because he owned the bank. By the time Jack paid for everything he needed on a weekly basis he was broke or in debt, and seemed to never get ahead.

George's instincts were right. He knew if he put money in front of Jack, he would chase after it, and never look inside for his natural gifts and talents. George's trick worked to perfection and Jack never learned to look for his hidden treasures within.

As time passed Jack married, had children and they, too, learned the ways of chasing money. For generations each family forwent discovering their hidden gifts and instead became chasers of money. George and his family, on the other hand, became wealthy and wealthier. Their riches were too great to be counted.

The Powerful Ones had done one very exceptional thing concerning the special powers they had placed inside of Jack. The same gifts that Jack possessed would be passed down from generation to generation, in hopes that the secret would someday be discovered.

ZENITH

ZENITH, FROM CHALDRON

Special people had extraordinary powers on the planet Chaldron. Some could move things with their minds, while others could read thoughts, and some, they say, could even fly.

Zenith, the Seer, was born on the planet Chaldron.. Her mother, Garr, was a healer, and her father Froc, a shape-shifter. Her father had the ability to become anything he could see. The only things he could not become were natural elements, water, air, earth and fire. Children learned how to find and use their special gifts at a very early age on Chaldron. Zenith's gift as a seer let her see into the future. She could also see gifts buried inside people.

One day Zenith was traveling from Chaldron, on her way to Oppiset, located in the deep spaces of torrent, and felt an odd pain in her heart. She had felt that pain many, many years ago, and knew immediately what it was. It was the pain of Gift-bearers whose powers are trapped inside them. Zenith could feel the energy of the hidden talents desperately wanting to be discovered and put to use. Zenith knew she had to stop what she was doing and go help those in need.

When Zenith landed her ship and began to walk through the town she noticed something strange. Many in the town had special gifts buried inside their beings, but for some reason they were not using them. To her amazement the gift-bearers were poor, while those without great gifts were rich.

Zenith wanted to tell the gift-bearers how special they were but she knew they would not believe her. She had to create a way to help them discover their treasures within. She thought for a moment and soon a plan came to her mind.

Signs appeared all over the town advertising a free class. "Anyone taking this class will become wealthy and live a grand life!" the sign read. Although everyone in the town saw the sign, only a few attended the class. People from the town had heard rumors about Zenith and her great powers but none had actually seen her. Awe and fear spread through the town, which caused many to stay away.-

On the appointed day, several students showed up for class. Zenith greeted them, and began training on how to identify their special gifts and talents. After a few weeks of training, Zenith made an announcement to her students, "You must go out into the land and take nothing with you!" The only things you will need are the special words I will give you before you depart. "Believe them and act on them, and great success will be yours," she said.

"There is one thing you must do to make your dreams come true," she said. All eyes were on Zenith. "What must we do?" asked an eager student. "You must believe," responded Zenith. "Believe in what?" an inspired student asked. "Believe in the things you cannot see," said Zenith.

"There will be times when things appear their darkest and you feel like you've lost your way. There will be times when doors are closed to you and you will think you are on the wrong path. There will be times when you are overcome with fear and doubt, but you must keep the faith and forge ahead," she said.

When times appear the bleakest, it is then, your belief must be the strongest," said Zenith. Each of the students understood and nodded their heads in agreement. "Repeat after me," stated Zenith. "No matter what I see with my eyes, I will believe in myself and my gifts. I will not be denied. I will never give up. And, in the end I will reach my destination because I BELIEVE," she exclaimed! Each student did as instructed and repeated the words.

Ten students went out into the world taking nothing but the clothes on their backs. Zenith whispered unique words in their ears. Somehow those words made each of them feel great and powerful. That power began to stir and awaken their hidden gifts.

Each person they met could tell they were special and began offering them favor. Complete strangers took them into their homes and cared for them. Many of Zenith's former students were given offers to speak for pay, while others were placed in powerful jobs and attracted great abundance.

The Secret Words

Before long, all of the students were very wealthy and well-known throughout the lands. Word spread of their successes and others sought Zenith to learn her secrets and the secret of the magic words she spoke to the students before they departed on their life's journey.

Zenith knew most people would not believe the secret words she whispered. The people had chased money so long they barely noticed the gifts inside them. If they knew the true value of the gifts stored inside them, they would stop chasing money and start working on developing their treasures within.

Zenith used her special powers to see into the future. What she saw made her heart-ache again. If she stayed in the town and helped free the gift-bearers, those who made money off their talents would soon hate her and put her to death. She knew she would have to leave soon but before she left she wrote these special words on a tablet," **To Who Will Believe; You, Too, Shall Be made Free.**"

She added instructions to her magic words." Read these words three times a day for 30 days. Read them in the morning, in the afternoon and before you go to bed at night. You must never miss a time, for the words must become part of your being. Once these words become a part of you, they will destroy the bad things you have learned and awaken the special gifts buried deep inside of you. At the end of the 30 days, your uniqueness will be revealed and your life will never be the same."

Zenith's Secret Words

I came into this world with riches buried inside me. It is up to me to seek those buried riches every day and bring them forth. The riches buried inside me are powerful and priceless. I believe in them because I believe in me and I am a miracle. My riches buried inside me are more precious than diamonds, rubies or any amount of money. I own the riches inside me and no one can take them away from me.

Today, I awaken to my true power and today I know who I am.

My talent is my money and no one can take my gift away from me. The more I develop my gift the more I increase my self-value. The more I increase my self-value the more wealth I will attract into my life. I alone control how well I hone my gifts and talents, and I alone determine my place in life. Today I work hard on discovering and developing my hidden powers and move a step closer to living the great life I am intended to live.

Today, I take control of my future and prepare myself for success and greatness!

Today, I will look for ways to be happy, I will be positive and helpful to others. When people see me they will want to be around me. Because I am friendly, others will want to be my friend. I understand I have everything I need inside me to become great and wealthy.

Today, I put away from me the fear of not being enough.

Today I will gather information and fill my mind with powerful thoughts. I will remain focused on what is in front of me and only connect with people seeking their own special gifts. Today, I will stop looking outside of me for riches and vow to only look inside. For my treasures are in me and from them, great wealth and power are mine!

Today, I am free. Today, I am strong. Today, I am great! – Today I know that, "I AM THE MONEY!"

Chapter Nine

A CHANGE OF HEART

One day the King called The Powerful Ones to his chambers. He had a special mission for them. He wanted them to create a plan to help Jack's children find their way to wealth and abundance, and save them from a life of hardship and poverty.

Using his omnipresent powers the King checked in on Jack and his family. Many times the sight of their struggle was too much for him to bear. Often, he considered calling his family home but decided against it. This time was different. "I am tired of seeing my grandchildren live such poor lives," said the King. "Go down and help them find their way."

The Powerful Ones looked at each other and came into agreement. Great care would have to be taken; an exceptional child would have to be chosen to fulfill such a special mission. Each knew there was no turning back.

The King had spoken and the King's will must be done. No words were exchanged but each knew where they had to go and what they had to do. Into the forbidden cave they would journey in search of the fated one

Most had heard rumors of the Cave of Whispers, but no living mortal had actually visited it. Matorius, the ancient dreaded soldier from the planet Dallies, responsible for the deaths of 5,000 men was said to occupy the cave along with the spirits of the deadliest warriors to have ever existed. The prize they guarded was precious cargo, spirits and secrets from the past and future.

With a bow to the King The Powerful Ones disappeared into thin air, on their way to the city of Nadar. There, they would seek out The Book of Lives, located in the Cave of Whispers.

The Cave was guarded by Metharian, a large multi-headed war beast. Metharian possessed a roar so mighty it could shatter the bones of men. His weight was comparable to a mountain, yet he could out maneuver any opponent. Each head on his massive frame operated independently adding to the terror his presence instilled in any who encountered him.

The Powerful Ones approached the cave and released a vibration that caused the massive cave wall to part and open. The ground trembled at the weight of the cave door and small rocks and boulders tumbled from the side of the mountain, down to the mouth of the cavern.

Metharian let out a death-threatening roar and turned to devour the intruders. Fire leaped from his eyes and mouth, as he prepared to defend <u>The Book of Lives.</u>

"It is us, old friend," was the message The Powerful Ones sent to the heart of Metharian. In an instance, the large beast knelt his monstrous body low and made way for The Powerful Ones to pass. As they passed, each man touched the servant-beast and sent messages of love to him. Metharian growled, this time lovingly to them, and wagged, what resembled a tail.

The men traveled deep into the cave to a place that held no light. Into the place of triple darkness they journeyed, guided only by some hidden compass buried inside each of them. The murmurings of a thousand ancient voices could be heard inside the darkness. The voices were ancient, cruel and withered. Some sounded like hissing more than voices. Only those shielded by the blood of Fatham, God of Thunder could withstand the hideous torment of the utterings, and gain entrance into the depth of the hollow.

The Powerful Ones, Uthor, Authurius and Dominacus, each wore the revered seal, and were protected by the sacred blood. The warrior spirits knew well of the supreme trio and challenged their entry, they dared not.

"We seek the one who can understand that which has not been understood," whispered Authurius." The whispering voices began speaking faster, as if in a panic, then without warning, a hush fell over the cave.

One mighty voice, so ancient it sounded more like gravel than a human voice ... spoke.

"There!" stated the voice.

"Look to see – he is there ... the one, you seek," the voice spoke again.

A single ray of light penetrated from the top of the cave to a spot on the cave's floor. The light beamed the most beautiful shades of blue and white. The ray of light was alive, and its energy spoke to the men. The Powerful Ones followed the energy of the light and bent to see what it revealed.

There on the ground, was the face of a boy. The Powerful Ones joined hands and spoke again to the voices in the cave.

"Show us!" said Uthor.

The picture of the boy shimmied and sprouted from the floor. The full grown image of the boy stood before The Powerful Ones. As The Powerful Ones looked into his eyes, the life of the chosen child flashed before them.

Each man was able to see the full capability of the boy. They could feel his heart and understand the workings of his mind. His unique set of talents made him different than all others, and he could be molded to handle a great task. "What is his name?" asked Dominacus. "Michael," said the voice of the ancient one.

The Powerful Ones sent a message of thanks to the ancient ones, and began their trek out of the cave. Back through the triple darkness and back to where Metharian waited. Metharian let out a cave-shaking roar as they approached.

"Goodbye old friend," spoke the men to his heart, each reaching out his hand to touch Metharian's bowed heads.

The cave opened, momentarily letting in the bright sunlight of the outside world. Utor, Authurius and Dominacus were happy to have found the chosen one and equally delighted to be on their way to meet him.

Chapter Ten

THE MESSAGE

Michael was a special child. He had a sparkle in his eyes. His energy was different than his brothers and sisters and at times he saw things happen before they occurred. By the time Michael was nine years old, family and friends knew he would be somebody when he grew up. Michael was destined to do amazing things.

Michael loved to be alone. He enjoyed his own company. Being alone gave him time to think and create a greater life by using his imagination. Sometimes he would journey to other planets in his mind, and create great and wonderful inventions. Michael could feel something powerful inside him; he, too, knew he was special but how very special, not even he could imagine.

One sunny day as he walked down the gravel road leading to his house, he was lost, deep in thought. In his mind, he saw huge buildings and flying machines. As he walked, he pretended to be the pilot of one of his flying machines. His flying machine would fly outside his window at his home and only he could make it fly. He smiled to himself. "One day my dream will come true," he thought to himself.

Michael jumped and screamed as he looked at his arm and saw a bumblebee about to sting him. He swung his arm frantically, desperately trying to rid his arm of the attacker. He swung his arm so hard he lost his balance and fell to the ground, hitting his head on a small stone.

He sat on the ground for a moment, looking at his arm to see if the bee had stung him. He was happy when he discovered he had not been stung. He got up to his feet and looked to see if anyone had seen his fall. As he stood and peered in the direction of his home, about 100 feet in front of him, stood three tall figures.

The sun was blazing hot. The heat caused waves of hot energy to form in the air. Michael wiped his brow and eyes, and tried to focus on the figures. No one walked on this path much except for him, his brothers and sisters. After blinking a few more times, he could see the figures were real.

"Come, young Michael," said the voice. Michael was startled, he could hear the voice but not with his ears. The voice was talking to him in his mind. "Be not afraid. There is nothing to fear," the voice said. Again, the voice was speaking to him inside his mind. Michael was not afraid. The voice was very comforting and somehow familiar. It sounded like the voice he had heard before, telling him of things to come before they happened.

Michael stopped in the middle of the road and looked at the three figures. Each wore a white robe. Each was very tall and the hood over their heads revealed no faces, only black empty spaces.

The Powerful Ones could feel Michael's questions and sent him a message of total love through their energy. Michael's heart received the signal and tears came to his eyes. The feelings of love were so strong, that Michael could not resist walking toward The Powerful Ones.

As he got close enough to see them clearly, a great light appeared around them. The glow created a halo that completely covered all three. The light was the color of the sun, and was radiant and very bright. Michael covered his eyes for a moment and tried to adjust his vision so he could see them, but when he opened his eyes, to his amazement, they were gone.

The Chosen One

"You are chosen," said the voice in his head. "Great and magnificent things will you do. Be not afraid, for we are with you and we will never leave you," said the voice of Authurius. For a moment, Michael could not move. His

eyes could not believe what he just saw, and his mind was on fire, still recalling the sound of the voices in his head.

He wondered how they were able to talk to him without moving their lips. "Am I dreaming?" he thought to himself. "How would anybody believe me?" he wondered. As quickly as he pondered the questions, the voice returned. "This message is for you and you alone, Michael. Share it with no one. You will create great things and by doing so, free many. For the time being, you must keep this information to yourself," said Uthor.

Again, Michael was dazed. What was he to keep to himself? Who would believe him anyway? The fact that he lived most of his life in his imagination would make people think it was just another of his wild fantasies, but this time there was proof.

Something lay on the ground in front of him, something square and flat. Was this another illusion and was his mind truly playing tricks on him, or was the object real? Michael walked over to the square lying on the ground and noticed it was a book. Michael bent down and picked the book up. It was covered with dust so he used his shirt to wipe it off. Jack and the Sly Fox, was written on the front cover.

Chapter Eleven

THE JOURNEY HOME BEGINS

The book was magical! It vibrated as he held it in his hands. Michael's heart was beating fast, and somehow he knew this was no ordinary book. His little legs could barely keep up with how fast his mind wanted them to carry him home. Straight to his secret hiding place he headed. He and his newly found special book.

Long ago, Michael had created a secret hiding place. His hiding place was high in a Sycamore Tree. He had stacked milk crates and nailed wood planks into the side of the tree so he could reach the lowest branch and pull himself up. On the branch he fastened old worn out pillows, he had taken from the house, to make his stay comfortable and enjoyable. This was his special hiding place, for him and him alone.

He hesitated a moment before opening the cover. He wanted to take in the beauty of the book. Its edges were golden, made from what appeared to be real gold. The letters on the book pulsated, one by one, when Michael ran his fingers across them. He could not explain the material the letters were made from because he had never felt material like that before. The book felt like joy, happiness, power and peace all wrapped together, and Michael felt a great warmth on the inside, when he held it.

The sun was still high in the sky when Michael opened the cover of his magical book. The book vibrated as he held it in his hands. This was a special book, and Michael could tell it wasn't from this world.

The first thing he saw when he opened the cover was a message to the reader. "My son, for so long I have missed you. I have missed the sweetness of your voice, the sparkle in your eyes and the happiness I felt when you were around." "It is time for you to find your way home to me. It is time you discover who you are. Please do not take these words lightly, for they are your road map that will lead you to great discoveries and at last, back home to me. Always know, I am with you, as are The Powerful Ones you saw today on the path. I am waiting patiently for you to find the path and restore my family to me. I am with you always," the message was signed ... King Zerias.

Michael's heart was alive! He wondered, "Could the message be for him?" It must be, he thought. How else would the writer know about The Powerful Ones he saw on the path? "Who is King Zerias," he thought to himself and how does he know about me?" Deep inside, he knew the book and the words were meant for him. He couldn't explain how he knew, he just knew. Michael closed his eyes for a moment to take in all that had happened. With a deep breath, he steadied himself and began to read.

Michael read about the seven gifts, and how those gifts would bring great wealth, and abundance into his life. His mind raced as he learned about George and how he had tricked his great, great, great granddad into chasing money. Michael grew angry when he learned how his grandpa was to live a great life, but instead made George rich. Michael made up his mind that moment that he would never chase money. Instead he would find his special gifts and use them to set his family free and bring them back home to King Zerias. Again, how he was going to do that he did not know but something inside made him believe it would be done.

Chapter Twelve

THE FIRST GIFT - AWARENESS

Michael did as The Powerful Ones told him and never shared his secret with anyone. He began his new journey in search of the hidden gifts inside him. "Where do I begin?" he asked out loud to no one in particular. "With the first gift," responded the voice in his head.

The first gift was **Awareness**, so that's where Michael began. Michael read about the Gift of Awareness and as he read, his inner gift began to stir. Miraculously, the world in front of him began to expand. Things he normally did not pay much attention, now seemed to jump out at him. The Gift of Awareness increased his ability to see the life in front of him as never before.

He was amazed by the fact the gift had been inside him all along. How could he have never known it was there, he thought to himself? He had used it in small doses but now it was alive and revealing to him secrets right before his eyes.

The first thing he became aware of was himself. He noticed he could think about something and know he was thinking. It was almost like having an out of body experience. He wasn't just capable of thinking; he knew he was thinking while he was doing so.

He grew aware of his moods and discovered he could change his mind if he wanted to. The Gift of Awareness began showing him things that otherwise went completely unnoticed. Michael could feel himself growing as he continued to become more aware.

Michael turned his attention to the other kids around him. He noticed how people hung around people just like them and did the things they saw others do. He became aware of how many kids his age didn't seem to think about the future they just thought about the moment. The Gift of Awareness showed him how the future is actually birthed out of the moment and that what he did today (or did not do) will show up in his life in the future.

Awareness opened his eyes to many things he never paid attention to before. People who don't want to succeed tend to find and hang with people who do not value success, he observed. While people who want to succeed tend to hang around people who value success. He also became aware of how hard it is to leave people alone who don't want to do better, because they want you to do the things they do, even if those things get you in trouble and cause you to fail.

Michael's awareness grew with each passing day and one day he learned the most valuable lesson. While talking in class, his teacher, Ms. Vandenbyer, scolded him and made him sit in the corner. This was far from the first time he had spent time away from the class, but this time it was different.

Using Awareness, Michael understood that his talking and not Ms. Vandenbyer had landed him in trouble. A light went off inside his head. "I can control what happens to me by controlling what I do!" Class was over and Ms. Vandenbyer stopped Michael at the door. Before she could scold him, he shared his revelation. "I am to blame for what happened in class today, Ms. Vandenbyer. Please forgive me," he said.

Ms. Vandenbyer looked hard at young Michael. She couldn't believe what she was hearing. She knew how clever he was, so she told him to explain. "It was my talking that got me into trouble, not you," he said. "From now on I will act responsibly and never interrupt your class again." Ms. Vandenbyer studied Michael and could tell he was being genuine. "I forgive you Michael and look forward to you doing better in my class," she said.

From that day on Michael used Awareness to control his actions. The times he thought about saying something out of line, he stopped himself and kept his mouth closed. Soon, other teachers were singing Michael's praises. His grades began to improve and he moved to the top of his class.

The Gift of Awareness kept showing Michael things he never saw before. He noticed how things kept repeating themselves. He noticed the people who did well in school, ended up with good paying jobs as adults, and those who didn't pay attention in school, paid for it as adults by living in poverty and lack.

Awareness helped Michael understand life. In an instant he recognized how short of a time a person remains a child, compared to how long a person is an adult. He somehow understood how hard adult life could be if a person misused their child years. Child years were supposed to be used to prepare for adulthood. Michael suddenly became aware of how few of his friends looked at life that way.

Most of his friends spent all their spare time playing and chasing girls. Few paid much attention to their education. Michael grew aware of the difference that existed between kids whose parents valued education verses the ones that did not. The parents who valued education insisted that their children do well in school, while parents who did not value education left it up to the kids to discover the power of education, on their own.

One day while walking home from school, The Powerful Ones appeared on the path. They wanted to know what Michael had learned using the Gift of Awareness. He told them all the things he had become aware of and how he used the Gift of Awareness to make all his decisions. The Powerful Ones were very pleased and sent Michael on his way.

Chapter Thirteen

THE SECOND GIFT – VISION

Michael's world and way of life is all he knew. He never traveled outside his town so he figured everybody lived as he did. Everybody knew each other and rarely did strangers enter the town. There was the Shepard Family who lived next door to him. Their house had a bad odor and the boys always picked fights with the other kids in town. Everybody made their living from farming, so there was really no need for fancy clothing. Life was pretty simple and Michael liked it that way.

That was until he read about the Gift of **Vision**. According to the book, by using the Gift of Vision, he could see far into the future, place himself in that picture he saw in his mind, and one day become the person he saw and live the life his Vision said he would unfold. The book said he could see himself doing something great, and if he held that picture in his mind, and move toward it with action, he would one day find himself doing the thing he foresaw.

By using Vision he could look beyond his current life and see other great possibilities. He could read books and not only dream about other places, but he could go visit them if he wanted to. Soon his curiosity began to mount and he often found himself dreaming of a bigger life and distant places.

Time passed and he continued to experiment with his Gift of Vision. One day Michael was in the school's band room and came across a saxophone. "Is this a hard instrument to learn?" he asked the band teacher. The instructor told him how any instrument can be learned if a person really wanted to learn it.

"That's what I'll do with my Vision," thought Michael. "I will use it to learn new things. I will see the thing I want to do and figure out a way to do it." Michael approached the teacher again and told him he wanted to learn how to play the saxophone. The teacher told him to come back the next day and he could start taking lessons.

Six months later the school's auditorium was full of people waiting to hear the band. Michael's mom and dad were there, too. The stage went black and the announcer came over the microphone, "Ladies and gentlemen, tonight we start out with a marvelous saxophone performance!"

The stage curtains slowly opened and the spotlight shined on a seated figure holding a saxophone.

As he rose to his feet so he could hit the high notes, his mother and father and all those watching recognized young Michael. At the end of his performance he bowed and the audience burst into thunderous applause. His vision had paid off. He saw an opportunity and made it happen. He didn't wait for someone to bring it to him; he went after the thing he wanted, and used his Vision to make it come true.

He trained himself to use his Vision in all things. He learned that if he saw something and wanted to make it happen, nothing could prevent him from having his dream, except him. He learned a great lesson. People who make it in life believe they can make it, see that they can make it, and just do it, while people who don't make it, stand back and wait for things to come to them. He decided from that day on he would be a member of the winner's group and not wait for good things to come to him, he would go get the great life he saw in his mind.

Chapter Fourteen

THE THIRD GIFT - UNIQUENESS

Michael read on and learned how The Powerful Ones had given Jack a unique set of fingerprints that separated him from every other human on the planet. The book told of the special power that came with being the one and only being on the entire Earth to possess this set of prints. "I am the one and only me!" he exclaimed to himself. He knew that meant something special. He knew, any time there was only one of something that meant it was very special. And, in this case, that one thing was him.

Michael looked at his fingerprint for the first time. He noticed the lines and how they appeared to make a circle on the tip of his finger. He observed the prints of his friends and found that each had different symbols on their hands. "I am the only one who has this symbol on my hand, mine is different from everyone else," said Michael to himself. "I am very special indeed!"

Michael's eyes were now open. He watched people who owned businesses and saw how they worked hard to set their business and services apart from the others. He noticed how those who strived to be the best loved being original. He also used his Gift of Awareness and became aware that although everyone comes to Earth original not many try to remain that way.

He looked around him and noticed how most people in school try to fit in. Nobody wants to be original. Everybody wants to blend in so, they don't stick out, he thought to himself. "That must be the secret," he said. "The people who make it in life create their own way and are unique, while those who aren't successful allow other's to dictate to them who they are or are not. They allow others who they consider stronger than them to choose the path they should take," he whispered out loud to himself.

"I am going to be like me," he said. He started to look for ways he could show his uniqueness. First, he decided he would work on his intelligence. He figured books are free so why not get as much information as possible? "When I speak I want people to know I am smart," he said.

One day, a group of kids approached him and asked him to run for Student body President. Although he never thought of doing such a thing, he agreed. He thought it would be a great way to show his uniqueness. The group put up signs and told people to vote for their guy, Michael.

The day arrived and each candidate had to give a speech in front of the entire student body. Michael was nervous. His hands were wet from sweat and he wondered what he had gotten himself into. He remembered his uniqueness and could feel his confidence return. His heart was beating fast and felt as if it was going to jump out of his chest. Soon it was his turn to speak.

A special confidence came over him when he heard the announcer call his name. All the other candidates stood behind the podium and delivered their speech but Michael grabbed the microphone and headed to the center of the stage, "I stand before you today, hoping you will stand behind me tomorrow, and back me with your vote in this election," Michael said to the audience.

When the final votes were counted, Michael had won. He was the new Student Body President. He didn't stop there. With every opportunity, he looked for ways to celebrate his uniqueness. Michael became the captain of his own life and took full control of where he was headed. He no longer let people talk him into doing things their way, he led by example and soon others began following his lead.

THE FOURTH GIFT - IMAGINATION

The chapter in the book Michael enjoyed most was **Imagination**. Since he spent most of his life living in that world, he felt he knew it well. The book talked about new inventions already put together, waiting for someone to discover them through the Gift of Imagination . "My new life is in my Imagination." That's what the book said," Michael said aloud. He was excited and ready to learn about the great gift "Imagination!"

Each day, Michael would take time and explore his Imagination looking for the new invention and his new life. The book said, "Things in the Imagination vibrated 100 times faster than things on Earth." Michael tried to use his mind to imagine what and how that worked.

One day, he was daydreaming and saw himself wearing new clothes and going to school feeling special. He started to dismiss the dream and move on and then thought about the book. 'Things move 100 times faster in the Imagination."

It was hard for Michael to understand what the book meant when it talked about things moving 100 times faster in the imagination realm. Then one day as he was walking home from school he encountered an occurrence that helped him understand. A horse with a sign on the side of it rode past Michael at top speed. Because Michael was walking slowly he could not read the sign. The horse was going too fast. Then he remembered a time he was riding a horse and rode next to a horse with a sign on its side. The fact he was traveling at the same speed as the horse (with the sign on its side) made it feel like they were standing still and it was easy to read what was on the sign.

That was the secret! To bring things to Earth from out of the imagination realm you have to speed up your energy to vibrate at the same speed of the idea. You then have to focus on the vision/thing residing in the imagination and slow it down to turn it from a vibration into a physical thing. He didn't know how he understood what he just said, he just knew he understood it, and that was good enough for him.

His dad had an old lawnmower he was trying to get rid of and Michael asked if he could have it. The mower had seen its best days. It was hard to crank and was rusted out along the wheels. When it finally started, it sounded more like a motorcycle than a lawnmower.

His dad asked him what he wanted to do with the lawnmower. Michael wasn't much of a handy man so his dad couldn't imagine him mowing lawns. "I have a project I want to do. Can I use it, Dad? Please?" It didn't take much for his dad to give in and let him use the mower. It was already full of gas, so Michael started out to fulfill his plan.

By the end of the day, Michael had cut 7 lawns. The neighbors were surprised to see him working so hard and happily paid him to cut their grass. Michael had made enough money to put more gas in the lawnmower and prepared himself to begin again the next day.

By week's end, Michael had cut enough lawns to buy what he wanted. He headed to town and marched into the local clothing store. "Hey Michael, what you doing in here?!" asked Barney. Barney was the son of the store owner. His gut fell over his belt like dough rising over a cake pan. "I'm coming to buy some new clothes," answered Michael. "You ain't got no money for no new clothes. Get on out of here, lying," Barney said.

Michael didn't listen to Barney. He walked right past him and picked out a nice shirt, belt, pants and even a new pair of casual shoes.

"What you want with those new clothes?" Barney prodded.

"I want to feel special," stated Michael.

Barney made some unpleasant, off-the-wall comment about how Michael was "Slow" and "Special."

"Where's your money?" asked Barney.

Michael reached into his pocket and pulled out enough money to pay for his new clothes.

"Man you ain't lying are you?" Barney said as his eyes grew wide.

"I told you I was gonna buy me some new clothes, didn't I?" Michael said.

"Yeah, I guess you did," said Barney.

Michael thanked Barney for the clothes and headed home.

Michael's dad met him at the door of the house.

"What ya got there in those bags Michael?" asked his dad.

"I bought me some new clothes," answered Michael

"Some new clothes -Where did you get the money" his dad asked, with a surprised look on his face?!

"I have been cutting lawns for the last couple of weeks and made the money," Michael said. He seemed to stand a little taller when he answered.

His dad looked down at his son and gave him a big smile.

"How did you know how to do that?" he asked.

Michael almost told him about the book and The Powerful Ones, but remembered their instructions.

"I saw it in my imagination, Dad. I saw myself wearing new clothes and then I went out and made it happen," stated Michael.

His dad was proud of him. He gave him a big bear hug and a loving pat on the back.

"You're going to be the big businessman one day, huh?" his dad said.

"Yep, I am!" said Michael. "I'm going to be the richest man in the world someday dad, you just wait and see!" Michael said.

Chapter Sixteen

THE FIFTH GIFT - CREATION

Michael had climbed to his secret hiding place in the tree many times, but this time he felt rushed. His mind was throbbing from the words he read in the book. The book had taught him so many things and by using the things he learned, he was growing in confidence and power.

Last night he dreamed an incredible dream. In his dream, he was a great King. In his Kingdom he had many servants, lots of land and his wealth could not be counted. He awoke from his dream full of energy, and each step he took was light as a feather.

He could hardly wait to get to his special place so he could read about the next gift, the Gift of Creation. Somehow, he knew this gift was most special. His mind tried to imagine what the words would say, before he read them. Perched high above the ground in his secret hiding place, in the silence of the summer, Michael prepared his mind to take in the message.

"The Gift of Creation is the maker of worlds," is how the chapter started. The book talked about "Turning nothing into something," and how everything you see was built using the Gift of Creation. Michael's mind tried to understand the meaning of those words. "How can I make something appear out of nothing," he asked himself. "Maybe if I use my other gifts I can find the answer," he mused.

He thought of the Gift of Uniqueness and how his originality made him special, but that didn't answer the question. He tried to use his inner Vision and Imagination, but neither helped him answer the question he posed. Then, he quieted himself and used his Gift of Awareness and energy began to form inside of him.

He began to look around and became aware of the houses on his block. He then became aware of the horses pulling buggies. He even noticed the clothes he was wearing ... and then – "That's it!" he exclaimed. Everything is created using other things! Where no clothes existed before, by creating thread and sewing it in a pattern, now clothes exist. Where there was nothing there now is something.

The climb down from the tree was slow and thoughtful. He had to weigh the information he had learned. "I can make something appear, that wasn't? I must go to see how this special gift works. With this special power I can be great and have everything I ever wanted," thought young Michael.

His first creation was simple. He walked down to the ocean and watched as the giant waves crashed against the shore. "There," he said, pointing to a flat surface of sand, "Where there is nothing, I will make something." At once, he began carving out figures in the sand. Soon his carvings became mounds and those mounds became little castles.

When he had completed his creation, he stood back and admired his work. To him, it was a masterpiece, but more than that, it represented his first creation. "Where there was nothing, I have made something," he proudly exclaimed.

He wanted to see how the Gift of Creation could make him money, so he sat on the porch of his house and looked out into the open space. For hours, he sat motionless, allowing his gifts to seek out a way to use Creation to help him make money. Then, in a sudden burst of energy, he jumped to his feet.

"Dad, Dad, where are you?!" shouted Michael. His dad was asleep on the sofa. Michael rushed to the place where his dad slept and without thinking, woke him up.

"Michael, are you crazy? What is wrong with you?!!" asked his dad.

"Dad, I need your help! I want to make a lemonade stand," Michael shouted, barely able to contain himself.

"Why on Earth do you want to do that son?" asked his dad.

"I want to create something that attracts money to me, Dad," Michael explained.

Michael began building his lemonade stand out of the materials his dad gave him. He created a sign for his business that read, "Michael's Best Lemonade'" and placed it on the front of his stand. His first customers were his family and neighborhood friends. Because it was summertime and the temperature was very hot, others from around the neighborhood stopped by to buy a glass of Michael's ice cold lemonade. In a short amount of time, Michael's lemonade stand was making him lots of money.

One day, Michael was preparing to get his lemonade stand ready for business and a voice in his head said, "Look at your lemonade stand. What do you see?" "Where there was nothing, I have made something," Michael stated proudly. "Very good, Michael, Very good, indeed," said the voice in his head.

THE SIXTH GIFT - VOICE

People started looking at Michael differently. Something special was happening to him and folks took notice. New friends started coming around, some wanting to work with him so they, too, could make money. Some just wanted to be around him because to them, Michael was gifted.

Michael could feel the change in himself, as well. His confidence continued to grow. The world somehow looked different and he was the captain of his life. His gifts were growing, too. Each time he used one of his gifts, it grew in power. The more the gift grew, the clearer his vision became. And, the clearer his vision became, the more empowered he felt inside. That dynamic energy he felt on the inside was experienced by others who came around him.

Michael, again, sat in his special place above the ground, safe and secure, in his long ago created tree house. So much had happened since that fated day he saw The Powerful Ones and his life had changed in amazing ways.

For a moment, Michael stared into the open space and allowed his Gift of Awareness to focus on the smallest things he could find. By now he knew how many trees were in his area, how many houses, cars, people and even how many windows were on the houses in his neighborhood.

He turned his Awareness back to the book and started reading about finding his Voice. "It is only by using one's own Voice that the special gifts inside can fully be used," said the words in the book. Only by finding and using his own voice could he speak with power and command his other gifts, Michael thought to himself.

Michael began thinking of ways he could find his own Voice. He thought of the time he ran for Student Body President and how great he felt speaking in front of his peers. He thought of mowing the lawns and buying his own clothes. Then, he thought of creating the lemonade stand and how special it made him feel to create something and make his own money. Then it hit him!

"Finding my Voice means finding me," he stated to himself out loud. All his life he had used his words to say the things he learned from other people. When he was small he learned how to say words by listening to his mom, dad, brothers and sisters. He learned how to say other words, some not so good, by listening to kids at his school. He never thought much about the words he said, he just said them. He recognized how much he had learned from his teachers. He noticed that when he listened to them, and applied their teachings, his knowledge grew greater, and his voice became clearer.

To find his Voice, Michael had to begin listening to himself and only saying the things that represented who he really was. To do that, he had to figure out who he wanted to be. He liked the attention he got from people when he did good things, so he decided to apply himself to being a good person. "I want to be somebody who people look up to," he proudly said to himself!

The next day, Michael got up and walked into the kitchen where his mom and dad were having breakfast and asked his dad if he could wear one of his ties. His dad wanted to know why he wanted one of his ties. "I want to be a special person when I grow up, Dad, so I want to start dressing like one now," Michael said. His dad beamed with pride as he looked into the bright young face of his son. "I'll get you a tie in a moment, Son," said his dad.

Heads turned as Michael walked down the hallways of school. His classmates wanted to know why he was all dressed up. Some of the kids teased him and asked him if he was going to church or something but that didn't matter to Michael. He had made up his mind that he was on his way to becoming someone great.

"You look so handsome, Michael," said Ms. Vandebyer. Michael thanked her and took his seat. Michael looked around and caught the stares of a couple of girls. He blushed and quickly turned away. The bell rang and he rose to leave. "You sure look nice, Michael," said Ellen Russell. Michael managed to quiet his racing heart long enough to thank her for the compliment.

Michael liked the way he felt and the positive attention he received when he dressed up so he continued to do so. Soon, people expected him to look sharp and on the days he didn't, they asked why. His popularity grew and when he spoke, people listened. At the end of the school year, Michael was voted, "Most Likely to Succeed."

Michael became a leader. His voice was strong and people knew when he said he was going to do something, he truly meant what he said. His actions followed his words and people knew they could depend on him. His learned to use his Gift of Voice to command his other gifts. All he had to do was command them, and when instructed to do something, each gift responded, "Yes Master." Michael had truly become the master of his gifts and the director of his life.

By finding himself, Michael found his Voice. By sticking to his word, others began trusting his voice. By not being afraid to take risks and to lead, people counted on him for direction. And, as time went on, Michael's voice became one of the most powerful young voices of them all.

Chapter Eighteen

THE SEVENTH GIFT - LOVE

Michael didn't want the book to be over, so he waited awhile before reading about the final gift. Something inside him knew the last gift would be the greatest. Each day he walked past the book, looking at it, and thinking about the great things he had learned.

The day came when he could wait no longer. The booked called to him, "It's time to read me," it seemed to say. He gently picked up the book and placed it on his lap as he sat on his bed. The book had become his friend, and he felt that if he finished it, it would somehow leave him.

"I am with you always," whispered the voice inside his head. His heart beat faster and he was filled with great warmth. "You have been chosen to do a great work and you have done well in understanding the things you have learned," said the voice. "This last gift will make you most powerful. Read on and you will see." The voice said.

Michael did as the voice commanded and learned about the Gift of Love. "Love your brother as you love yourself, and love those who treat you badly," were written in the book. Michael tried hard to understand those writings but his mind could not comprehend.

Night time came and Michael's mind was restless from all the reading he had done that day. He climbed into bed and tried to fall asleep, but sleep he could not find. He tossed and turned, and his mind stayed on the teachings of the book. "I cannot understand!" he yelled aloud as he pulled the covers over his head and lie silently under his covers.

Only moments had passed from his outburst, yet he could see light through his bed covers. "How could it be daytime?" he thought. He had just gone to bed. He slowly removed the covers from around his head and looked out into his room. What he saw startled him for a moment but only for a moment.

Standing in his room were Uthor, Dominacus and Authurius, covered in radiant light. One of The Powerful Ones spoke to Michael without talking. Michael could hear Dominacus' voice in his mind. "Come, young Michael. We have much to show you." The love of The Powerful Ones was great upon young Michael. He could tell they loved him and he felt no fear of them.

The Journey to Love

He rose from his bed and went to The Powerful Ones. As he walked toward them the room disappeared. The next thing he knew he was standing in a hospital room watching a mother hold a newborn child. The Powerful Ones were standing next to him and talked to him in his mind. "The new child is innocent. He is full of love. Do you see the love around him, Michael?" said Authurius.

Michael could see the rays of love coming from the newborn baby. He had never seen anything like that before. The baby was surrounded in pure love and the love was the color of the sun. Michael was surprised. No one else in the room seemed to see the beautiful light radiating from the child. "Earth-eyes cannot see the light. It would blind them," said Uthor.

The mother was also covered in love. Not like the baby, but love from the baby. "You were like that, too, when you first came here, Michael," said the Dominacus, and somehow Michael understood.

In an instant, the room was gone and Michael was standing in a grocery store. Again, The Powerful Ones were at his side. The door of the store opened wide and through it, came a man holding a gun. "Give me all your money!" the man said to the store clerk, holding the gun inches from the clerk's face. The store attendant shook with fear. "Please don't kill me," he pleaded with the gunman, as he handed him the store's money.

The gunman, after receiving the money, hit the attendant in the head with the butt of his gun and ran out of the store. The store clerk grabbed his head as blood gushed from his wound and he fell to the ground. Michael was afraid and sad for the store clerk. "What does all this mean?" he asked The Powerful Ones.

"Did you see the little boy covered in love?" asked Authurius. "Are you talking about the man carrying the gun who just hit the man in the head and robbed him of his money?" asked Michael. "Yes," said Authurius. Did you see the little baby covered in love?" Authurius repeated the question.

"No," answered Michael. "All I saw was an evil man who hurt that other man and took his money!" The next minute, Michael was traveling through time. He could not tell if he was moving or standing still. Pictures and time flashed before him at a fast pace. The pictures and times were the baby's life. The baby he saw at the hospital. The baby who came to Earth covered in pure love.

Michael watched as the baby was brought home from the hospital and placed in his home. He listened as the baby's father cussed and beat the baby's mom. The frames of the vision moved very fast, but he could feel what the baby felt as his little spirit became battered and bruised. Then, Michael noticed something that hurt him deeply; the rays of love once covering the baby slowly began to die out.

The Powerful Ones stood closer to Michael and covered him with their love. He could feel the energy of their love for him and it made him feel safe. All through the night he was shown life after life of babies who came to Earth covered with pure love. He witnessed how life after life, each baby's little light was put out by the harshness of living.

Understanding Love

"We knew you could not understand why you should love everyone. We knew we had to show you," said Uthor. Tears were streaming down Michael's face; he could not erase the vision he saw. "Everybody comes to Earth full of love," he thought to himself, "and the ways of the world turn them into something they were not meant to be." Now he understood why and how to truly love.

The sunlight dancing through the window awoke Michael. He looked around for The Powerful Ones but they were gone. He sat up in his bed, his mind somehow relaxed and peaceful. The images of the night before were still vivid in his mind, yet somehow love had replaced the images of pain.

"Today I will love everybody like the newborn baby," he said out loud. He jumped from his bed and ran downstairs to his mom and dad. His face was aglow and his eyes were alive. His dad sat at the kitchen table reading the morning newspaper. Michael grabbed his dad around the neck with both arms and kissed his face, then buried his head deep into his father's chest. "I love you, Dad," he said.

His mother turned around from the kitchen sink to see what all the fuss was about. Michael ran to her, gave her a big hug and said, "I love you so much, Mom!" As he held onto his mother she shot a confused look over to his dad. "We love you, too, Son, what has gotten into you this morning," asked his mom? Again, Michael thought of telling them about the book but remembered his instructions. "I just wanted to tell you both how much I love you, that's all," said Michael.

Michael hurried and got dressed and headed to school. Along the way he passed people and looked in their faces. A homeless man passed by him and he looked into the man's face. He looked to see if he could catch a glimpse of the baby covered in pure love. To his amazement he could see a small flicker of light still remaining in the homeless man's eyes. The man noticed Michael's look and seemed to know his thoughts. He winked at Michael and Michael smiled, and winked back.

Michael's heart began to change as he learned to look for the love in each person he met. He realized he, too, was that baby covered in pure love and each day learned to re-connect with his love within.

Michael grew in love and learned how to use the greatest gift known to man. He soon realized how little people used the Gift of Love. He also learned how much people really want love. Even the hardest people want to be loved, he discovered. He finally came to understand that if you continue to love someone though they treat you unkind, your love will eventually melt the coldest of hearts. Michael's greatness increased one hundred fold due to learning about and using the most powerful gift of them all ... the Gift of Love.

Chapter Ninteen

MICHAEL THE GREAT!

As Michael grew in age his popularity grew along with it. Strangers from miles around sought him out to hear his words. Word spread about the loving energy that seemed to surround young Michael and rumor had it he had actually healed a man by shaking his hand. No one can say if the rumor is true but the man who was healed swears by it to this day.

Michael began receiving gifts and money from those who sought out his counsel. His words were profound and his insights revealing. By using love he was able to speak to the heart of anyone he encountered. And, when a person experienced his genuine love, their heart reacted and opened up to him.

"Love is the greatest gift of all," he told his listeners. "Each of us came here covered in pure love. If only you could have seen yourself as a baby and your eyes could have been gifted to see the love you were surrounded by, then you would know who you really are," said Michael to the crowd of listeners.

"From this day forth, I want each of you to look for the baby covered in pure love in each and every one you meet and in yourselves. It may be hard to see the love in some because life has been hard to them and they have grown cold and hard. But, if you use your own Gift of Love and be patient you will discover the love buried deep inside of them" said Michael.

Michael grew to be the wealthiest man in the world. His land stretched for miles and miles and his workers numbered in the thousands. He used his money for good and helped countless families in need. "The Gift of Love is the gift that keeps on giving," he was known to say.

Chapter Twenty

SUNDOWN

Michael sat in the orchard of one of his many mansions and looked out over his expansive acreage. Many years had passed since his walk down the dusty trail and his encounter with The Powerful Ones. His life had changed so much since he learned about his special gifts.

Thousands had come to him and many had used his lessons and changed their lives. As he looked back over his years, Michael noticed the difference between those who succeeded and those who failed. Those who succeeded desired to be winners and were quick to look inside themselves for their special gifts.

The winners, upon finding their gifts, practiced relentlessly and used the gifts to make their dreams come true. And, although some did not reach the height of their dreams, all who tried, lived a greater life than those who did not.

Those who did not win did not work on their natural gifts and talents. Although they enjoyed the information, they never practiced the things they learned. Michael also noticed those who did not win, gravitated toward others who did not win, and found solace in the unions.

Chapter Twenty One

THE FINAL MISSION

The sun beat down on Michael as he sat in his favorite deep-padded chair. He closed his eyes and allowed himself to fully take in the gentle breeze coming through his window. The sun felt comforting as it beamed down on his sun-baked face.

His mind was restless as it had been in the past when he knew there was something he was supposed to do. He tossed and turned from one side of the chair to the other, desperately trying to figure out why he could not find peace. The ottoman on which his feet rested did little to comfort him. Then, a voice appeared in his mind, "There is one more thing for you to do," said the voice.

It had been a long time since he heard that voice, yet it was as familiar as the sun-filled sky he had stared into for all the years of his life. "What must I do?" he asked the voice in his head. The voice shared the greatest vision of all. Michael had learned long ago to trust the voice and do what it asked. Michael's well-kept hands began to tremble slightly as he took in the enormity of the mission.

When the voice finished, Michael was sitting up straight in his favorite chair. His restlessness gone, replaced by excitement and high energy. His mind, forgetting the age of his weathered old legs sent a long forgotten message of youthfulness to them and he leap from his chair onto his feet.

For the moment, his mind was alive and on fire. His walking cane, used to hold his heavy frame was unnecessary as he hurried into his office and onto his telephone. He arranged meetings with his most powerful advisors and told them to put together a team of the best architects in the land. He also told them to scour the land and find him the best scholars money could buy.

"What is it, Michael? What are you about to create?" asked one of his councilmen. "I am about to build the grandest school this world has ever seen!" Michael stated excitedly.

The voice had shown Michael a great vision. In the vision, the world looked like a picture out of a science fiction movie. In the new world, people used their gifts to create the desires of their heart. No longer were human beings chasing money. Instead, they learned about their inner-gifts and made their wildest dreams come true.

His final mission was to build a school where kids could learn about their special gifts. He knew it would take the right words to convince them of how special they are, but he struggled to imagine what those right words should be. Then, in an instant, he knew what he must do.

AN OLD FRIEND

He walked into his massive library filled with books and looked around. Plato, Socrates, Aristotle and many of the great minds rested on the shelves. Michael was proud of his book collection. He loved how books let his mind escape to other places, without having to leave his home.

He looked around the book-filled room and located the special book he was looking for. Although it looked like a regular book it was special. Michael reached out his hand and pulled the book toward him. The sound of a latch releasing could be heard as the wall of the library opened, revealing a hidden chamber. Light shined through the entryway of the chamber and Michael opened the door wider, and walked in.

The chamber was expansive. Rubies, diamonds, and

gold filled the room, and the energy of their rare substance glimmered, danced and cast mighty rays of the most brilliant colors throughout the room.

As Michael studied his vast collection of priceless heirlooms, he seemed unimpressed by the great collection. Instead, his eye sought something else, something simpler, yet magnanimous. He sought the knowledge of an old friend.

At last, he walked over to a table made of marble and granite and opened its drawer. Inside, he found what he had been seeking. It had been a long time since he held it and before doing so, he looked upon it for a time. <u>Jack and the Sly Fox</u>, the title read. "This is it," he thought to himself. "Upon this book I will build my school."

Michael reached down and gently picked up the book. He held it next to his heart and took a moment to feel its energy. His eyes glistened and came to life as he thought of who he had become as a result of the knowledge housed in this small book.

He wondered why he was chosen for such an extraordinary task. He was no one of merit. He didn't come from a wealthy family. "Why me?" he thought to himself. "From the smallest comes the largest, Michael," said the voice in his head. "You were created for this great task and you have done your job well," the voice said.

Chapter
Twenty Three

THE SCHOOL

The architects developed the blueprints of the new school and presented them to Michael. Never had he seen such a magnificent layout of buildings. Each building was masterfully crafted, spacious and unique. It was of utmost importance that each building conveys a feeling of adventure, excitement, awe, and amazement. Michael had insisted and given stern orders to create an atmosphere conducive to drawing out the hidden gifts of the students.

Scholar after scholar visited Michael and sat and listened as he taught them the ways of the book. The scholars were great in knowledge, but even their wisdom had to bow to the wisdom of The Powerful Ones. After much review, Michael sent them away to reflect on how best to use the teachings of the book to bring each new student's gifts to life.

Word traveled throughout the land that Michael was building a special school. People came from miles away forming long lines and desperately seeking ways to sign up their children. If Michael were prepared to share the knowledge that made him so great, they would gladly pay any price to have their children learn from the wealthiest man in the world.

Finally the day came and the doors of the school opened. Children with eager faces chattered among themselves and the sound of their voices filled the hallways. This school was different. Instead of learning about reading, writing and arithmetic (at the beginning), they learned about who they were and received instruction on how to identify, and develop their unique gifts and talents.

As a result of the specialized training each student received, a different energy filled the classrooms, hallways, and cafeteria. Differences were celebrated as each student learned of the power of Uniqueness. The campus vibrated with intensity as students began to develop and use their hidden gifts and talents.

By the time reading, writing and arithmetic were introduced to the students their well-defined sense of awareness aided them in understanding the relevance of the disciplines. Student engagement was high and teachers looked forward to coming to work. "Self-

Development Equals Wealth-Development," became the mantra of the school.

Each student was treated as an individual and underwent a time of observation and discovery. The teachers were taught to look for each child's special gifts and upon finding the gifts they were instructed how to draw them out. Hands eagerly rose to answer questions well into the latter years of schooling, for each child.

Michael kept close watch over the progress of the school and the students. He demanded up-to-date information of how the process was working and if the students were receptive to the training. He was pleased as he learned about the new inventions the children were creating. Most of all, he was pleased to hear how they were learning to love themselves and each other.

HOMECOMING

Michael's health began to wane. He had lived a long life and was happy about all he had accomplished. His breathing grew heavy and he could tell his final days were upon him. One night, while lying in bed, the voice returned in his mind, "Michael, it's time to come home."

Michael struggled to sit up but his weary body rebelled, and did not cooperate. Suddenly, the brightest light appeared in his room. He recognized The Powerful Ones and was happy to see them again. Standing with them in the light was another figure. "Michael, there is someone here to see you," said Authurius.

The figure moved closer to Michael and as he did, Michael was filled with the greatest feeling of love he had ever experienced. Without warning, tears began streaming down Michael's face. The tears were not tears of sadness, but tears of pure joy. Never had Michael felt such a deep, consuming love. He closed his eyes and let the energy of the love fill his mind, body and soul.

"I have waited for this moment and now it is here," said the figure standing before him.

With his heart full of love Michael asked, "Who are you?"

"I am the King and the father of your distant grandfather. Please allow me to show you something," said the King.

In an instance, Michael was shown the past and how Jack had been deceived by George the Sly Fox. When the vision ended, Michael knew everything.

"You have done your job well. Now come and see the reward of your great work," said King Zerias.

Jack Returns Home

The room in which Michael lay a moment ago was gone. Enveloped in a massive wind, he was lifted high above the Earth. Although the wind surrounded him, his clothes remained unruffled. He could hear the sound of many voices singing inside the roaring wind. The voices of those singings were angelic, majestic and soothing. Never before had Michael heard songs or sounds as beautiful as these.

The wind stopped and he was on the shore of a great body of water. The water was so clear and beautiful he lost himself for a moment, staring into its vastness.

"Michael," said a familiar voice.

Michael turned to the voice and what he saw caught him by surprise. Thousands of smiling faces and sparkling eyes were looking back at him. They all seemed to know him and he could somehow feel a connection to each one of them. Oddly, they each appeared to look like him, too.

The Powerful Ones stood nearby and looked lovingly upon Michael.

"Who are they?" asked Michael.

"They are your family of the past," said Uthor.

In an instance, Michael somehow knew each person. His grandfather, great grandfather, great, great grandmother and so forth.

"How are they all here, and why?" asked Michael.

"You, Michael, you are why," said Dominacus.

Michael looked confused.

Dominacus continued ...

"The fact that you discovered and developed your natural gifts and learned how to love opened a door for all your family to return home to the Kingdom."

"Your work and discovery of your gifts paved the way for your entire family to come home. These people are your family. They have watched you and hoped for you. Because of you, they are now whole and able to return home."

Michael was then shown how the King had created a special place for the spirits of all the lost family members. It was a marvelous place and now those who were lost would live in harmony forever and ever.

There was movement in the crowd and a man walked toward Michael. The man's hair was beautiful silver. Not aged, but brilliant and alive. His love for Michael filled Michael's heart and he reached out his arms and embraced him. He spoke to Michael in his mind and Michael knew who he was.

"Hello, Michael, I am Jack, your distant grandfather. What began with me has ended with you."

One by one, each family member came to embrace Michael. Their love was the love of a parent who longed to rejoin with a long lost child. Soon, their love became one and the rays of light shined into the air like the rays of love surrounding the newborn babies.

The Powerful Ones appeared before the crowd and sent a message telling them it was time to go in. Each heart was alive with expectation of reuniting with the King. For so long they had waited for this very moment and the waiting was over. With outstretched arms, the King greeted each of his long lost children.

"Welcome home family! I love you all so very much. Come. I have much to show you," said the King.

Jack
& the Sly Fox

STUDY GUIDE
Putting Your Gifts to Work for You

Although, <u>Jack and the Sly Fox</u>, is not a true story, it does share many truths. The story is designed to help you discover your own special gifts and talents. Picture Michael and what he did to discover and use his special gifts. Follow his example and you too, will find your way to your special gifts.

When you find out you have a special gift, really take the time to learn how to use it. You may have to read the book more than once. It may take many times before you learn the secrets of your hidden gifts and talents.

Most people chase after money but not you. After you learn how to develop your gifts you will become like Michael, the opportunities, and money will be chasing you. You will be able to say, "I don't chase the money, the money chases me."

THE FIRST GIFT –
THE GIFT OF AWARENESS

Only one being on the planet would be awarded this special gift. Only humans could bear the Gift of Awareness. Awareness is a powerful gift. The gift is so powerful it can see itself. The person who has the Gift of Awareness is aware she is ... aware.

If you have the special Gift of Awareness, you will know. If you would like to see if you have this very amazing gift, try this exercise: Can you tell if you are thinking right now? If you are aware you are thinking, you have the powerful Gift of Awareness.

Now that you've discovered you possess one of the most extraordinary gifts on the planet, let's see what it can do. A great gift does you no good if you do not know how to operate it.

Try to see if you are aware of what mood you are in right now. Are you able to do that? See if you can become aware of your thoughts right now. Were you able to do that? If you were, the power of Awareness is working for you. All you have to do is direct it, and it will do the rest.

118

Use one of the choices below and write about how you can use the Gift of Awareness. You can become aware of you, someone else or a place. There is no wrong answer, so feel free to be as creative as you desire.

A. Yourself

B. Someone Else

C. Some place

Example: I am aware that my friend April likes to dress like me.

_____

_____

_____

_____

_____

_____

_____

_____

_____

Great! You have begun your journey to finding and using your gifts. Keep this book with you so you can look at what you wrote from time to time. Now that you know about your Gift of Awareness you can use it, on purpose, anytime you want to. You are its master and it is here to serve you.

Awareness and Wealth

"Some people see things as they are and ask why.
I see things as they can be and ask, why not?"
— Robert Kennedy, quoting George Bernard Shaw.

The Gift of Awareness enables you to be aware of what is and what is not. Bill Gates, the founder of Microsoft became aware of the need for computers and used that awareness to begin his study of programming. Elias Howe recognized women needed to be able to sew clothes faster and invented the sewing machine. Garrett Augustus Morgan saw the need for drivers to know whose turn it was at a traffic stop and invented the traffic light.

Use your Awareness now and try to become aware of something missing in today's society. Use your Gift of Awareness to help you identify something that could benefit your neighborhood, city or the world. When awareness is turned on, it uses its power to magnify your world. Once magnified, you can clearly see what you can do to build a better world. Building that better world will attract great wealth into your life.

Write down something you think could make the world a better place to live.

THE SECOND GIFT – THE GIFT OF VISION

The Powerful Ones knew Jack would need to see into the future if he was to create great amounts of wealth. They called on the Gift of Vision to help Jack see far and wide. With Vision, a person can see things that are not, as if they are.

Vision is a very powerful gift. You have this great gift you merely have to learn how to use it. Let's see if you have this precious gift. Can you remember a time you wanted something but didn't have the money to buy it? Do you remember what you did to finally get it? Try to remember the feeling you had when you saw yourself with the thing you wanted, before you got it.

Now, take a moment and remember how you felt when you finally got that thing you wanted so badly. Did you look at yourself in the mirror, while you were wearing it? Did you show it off to your friends? Were you proud that you had it?

Vision is what helped you see yourself having something before you actually had it. You saw a picture of what you wanted, in your mind. That's the Gift of Vision. The secret you must learn is how to use that special gift all the time. The Gift of Vision will help you obtain your greatest reward.

Use one of the choices below and write about how you can use the Gift of Vision. You can write about yourself, someone else or a place.

A. Yourself

B. Someone Else

C. Some place

_____

_____

_____

_____

_____

_____

_____

_____

_____

_____

_____

_____

_____

_____

_____

Vision, like Awareness, sits and waits for you to take control of it. Vision is always ready to work for you; you just have to tell it what you want it to do. It will look for a new life for you if you tell it to. It will show you a way to overcome a bad habit. The Gift of Vision acts as a light shining the way to your brighter future.

Visioning and Wealth

"Dream lofty dreams and as you dream, so shall you become," said author, James Allen. The powerful Gift of Vision helps you look ahead and prepare for things and times to come. When you turn on vision you will see the life you want to create and be able to see the moving parts necessary to create it.

Others can tell when a person of vision is in their presence. That person speaks of things to come and things he/she **will** do. By using Vision you see the scholarship you can have. You visit the college, fill out the application, and soon enter through the doors as a college student.

Vision sees the life you want to live and allows you to place yourself into the picture. The great thing about vision is you are allowed to see a picture as big as you want. Only you can limit how big your vision can be. The wealthy life you want can be yours if you learn to use Visioning.

Can you use the Gift of Vision to see the life you want to live and put you in the picture? Take a moment and write down the vision you see for yourself in the next 5 years.

_____

_____

_____

_____

_____

_____

_____

_____

_____

_____

_____

_____

_____

_____

_____

_____

_____

_____

_____

_____

THE THIRD GIFT –
THE GIFT OF UNIQUENESS

Authurius, Dominacus and Uthor understood the value of things. They knew the more there was of a thing, the less its value. They also knew the less there is of something, the more valuable it becomes. For that reason, they created and gave to Jack, the Gift of Uniqueness.

"We will make him the first, last, the one and only," said the Authurius. They placed a print in Jack's hand, gave him a special voice and special eyes that he alone possessed. They made Jack original, meaning there is none other exactly like him in the world. Never has been and never will be.

If you have a fingerprint you, too, have the extraordinary Gift of Uniqueness. Your eyes are original and your voice is, too. You are the first, last, the one, and only you. If no one has told you what that means or the great advantage it provides, it's time you understand its unique value.

The Gift of Uniqueness is an extraordinary gift. Try to see it this way: Any time there is only "One" of something, on

the planet, makes it very valuable. That's who you are. Take a moment and write how you can use uniqueness to create success in your life.

_____

_____

_____

_____

_____

_____

_____

_____

_____

_____

_____

_____

_____

_____

_____

_____

_____

_____

_____

_____

_____

Uniqueness and Wealth

Sometimes you may not feel very special. It is easy to want to fit in and feel like you belong. People around you can try to make you feel like you are odd, and you can start seeing yourself that way if you do not know who you are.

When you understand the power of your uniqueness you stop trying to fit in. Instead, you become proud of whom you are. You begin to realize you are just the way you are supposed to be and that makes you very beautiful. You are one of a kind; you're not supposed to be like anyone else but you.

It is not your external features that make you beautiful it is who you are on the inside that truly makes you shine. The moment you understand that fact is the moment you stop wishing your eyes and nose looked like someone else's. You begin to teach yourself how to love you and your very own uniqueness. When other's experience your love for your looks and love for self, they will desire to look and feel like you.

Have you ever noticed how people are attracted to celebrities? You may have a favorite rapper or singer. If you look closely, you will see how they use their uniqueness to gain popularity. Celebrities do everything they can to be different from everybody else. They use the Gift of

Uniqueness to show others how very special it is to be them. You can do that, too.

How can use your Gift of Uniqueness to make you stand out from the crowd and help you attract money into your life?

_____

_____

_____

_____

_____

_____

_____

_____

_____

_____

_____

_____

_____

_____

_____

_____

_____

_____

_____

THE FOURTH GIFT – THE GIFT OF IMAGINATION

"Imagination is your world
it's a preview of things to come,"
— Albert Einstein.

G reat inventions from the future were made available to Jack through the Gift of Imagination. If Jack would work hard to learn how his Gift of Imagination worked he would be able to download great ideas and witty inventions into his mind, and onto the planet. Those clever inventions would attract to him great wealth, abundance, and a prosperous life.

The secret to the Imagination was how fast energy moved. Every object in the imagination moves 100 times faster than the physical. Objects and future inventions were completely put together in the imagination, but Jack would have to focus all his attention on them if he were to bring them on to Earth.

"Imagination is your world. It's a preview of things to come," said scientist, Albert Einstein. Einstein was right;

he understood the fertility of the imagination realm. He had worked and played in it all his life and recognized the gifts stored in it were/are real.

Imagination is different than vision. Vision enables you to look at the future and create from what you see. Inventions are already put together in the Imagination, waiting for you to discover them, and bring them out.

You probably never took an imagination development class. Most people find out how to use their imagination accidentally. Those who discover the Gift of Imagination and learn how to use it, continue to discover great things. The rest of the world watches them, and wonders how they do it.

The Gift of Imagination is an adventurous gift. The gift allows you to see things that are already for you to bring to this planet. You can add to something already invented or bring something totally different (like Facebook) to Earth. Take a moment and try to use your Gift of Imagination and imagine something you can bring from your imagination world into this world. Be as creative as you want. Let your imagination run free.

_____

_____

_____

_____

_____

_____

_____

_____

_____

_____

_____

_____

_____

_____

_____

_____

_____

_____

_____

_____

Imagination and Wealth

This book you are reading now was first in the author's imagination. The fact you are reading it means somebody paid money for it. All inventions in the imagination can be used for the advancement of mankind and to attract money.

Facebook existed in Mark Zuckerburg's mind (the founder of Facebook). Mark used his Gift of Imagination, to work hard and bring Facebook out of his mind onto this world. Facebook is now worth billions of dollars.

When you learn how to use the Gift of Imagination you, too, will be privy to great inventions. The first thing you must do is learn how it works. You may be walking along and a vision may pop in your head. The vision may be something the world, your school or your community needs. The more you think about it, the more the inner vision grows. Soon, you may find yourself talking to others about it.

You must be careful when sharing visions from your imagination with your friends. If you share the secret from your imagination with a doubting person or a person who doesn't understand how the imagination works, they may try to talk you out of going after your dream. Big dreams can be crushed by doubters and people who don't believe someone like you can accomplish such a great thing.

One final lesson: It is impossible for you to see something in your mind, completely put together, that cannot be created on Earth. Remember, airplanes and their ability to fly in the sky with people inside, were considered impossible at one time. Never forget the words Zenith gave to her the ten students, "You must believe."

Can you think of something you saw in your imagination that you wanted to create? If you did, write it down. Maybe you haven't taken time to listen to your imagination. If not, this is a great time to start listening closer for the great things your imagination has for you. How can you listen closer for what your imagination is trying to tell you? Take a few minutes, close your eyes and listen. Now, write your answer. You can answer either question.

_____

_____

_____

_____

_____

_____

_____

_____

_____

_____

_____

_____

_____

_____

_____

_____

THE FIFTH GIFT – THE GIFT OF CREATION

The fifth gift is the Gift of Creation. The Gift of Creation can help you create something out of nothing. You are, too, young to remember when people had to ride horses to get to where they wanted to go but that was how people used to travel.

There was a time where there were no tall buildings, no cell phones, no internet, and no television. Even the small things such as nails, paperclips and glue, at one time did not exist. All those things had to be created. How often do you think of creating something out of nothing?

Imagine if you wanted to build a house. The first thing you would need to know is how big of a house you want to build. You would then hire a developer or architect to draw the design/blueprint. You would then have a team of people bring the materials needed to build the building. You would watch over the process and soon your house would be built. Keep in mind; all the materials needed to complete the project had to be created by someone.

One day while driving to your newly built house you may recall the vacant lot that it once represented. You will remember each step leading up to the finished result. If you were to go back over the process leading up to your house being built, you will see how where there was nothing but an empty lot, now sits the house of your dreams. That is the power of Creation.

Take a moment and write down how you can use the Gift of Creation to create something out of nothing.

The Gift of Creation and Wealth

Remember, Jack used the Gift of Creation to build a lemonade stand and sell lemonade to make money. There are many other ways you can use Creation to attract wealth into your life.

Many young people use selling candy as a great means to attract money. They see the opportunity in their minds, ask their mom, dad or family member for the money to get started, and soon are on their way to running their own candy selling business.

You too, can use the Gift of Creation to create things that can attract wealth into your life. Start looking for positive ways to create things of value. The more care you put into the things you create the more valuable they will be to others. Soon you will be on your way to creating a business that you take care of and that takes care of you.

The world you live in was made possible by people who created the things you use on a day to day basis. Learn to look closer at the things you use and recognize that somebody created it. What can you create? How can you use the Gift of Creation to attract wealth into your life? Take a moment and write it down.

THE SIXTH GIFT – THE GIFT OF VOICE

*Y*ou voice controls your other gifts. Your voice is the general and your other gifts are the troops. When you speak you set energy in motion. Imagine a still body of water. Now, imagine taking your hand and pushing the water in a forward direction. Can you imagine the ripples and waves you would create from using your hand to move the water? What's even more interesting is the fact the water will not resist you. When your voice becomes strong enough your gifts will obey you.

Finding Your Voice

To find your own voice you have to find the "Real" you. To find the real you, you have to find your center. To find your center you have to quiet yourself, listen to your thoughts and try to discover your true values and beliefs. If you take the time to search yourself you will find your true self. To that person be true.

Many times we try to fit in. We may hang out with our friends and pick up some of their habits. We may experiment with a lot of different styles as we try to find the one that fits. Through it all, we must become comfortable with being who we are.

When you find your center, you will feel comfortable in your own skin. You will stop trying to please everybody and seek to please you, first. You will learn that being yourself is all you need to be and those who love you will love you just the way you are.

The best way to find the real you is to ask yourself, "What do I really believe in?" Really take a moment and listen for the answer to that question. Find a place where you can be still and hear the small voice within. Most people never ask themselves that question and therefore never find their authentic voice. Learn to observe your belief system and you will be on your way to finding your natural voice.

Great people have developed their voice to express their thoughts and ideas. Take a moment and write how you can use the Gift of Voice to help you become the great person you are meant to be.

_____

_____

_____

_____

_____

_____

_____

_____

_____

_____

_____

_____

_____

_____

Your Voice and Wealth

The marketplace is filled with people who make millions of dollars using their Gift of Voice . Rappers, authors, politicians, poets, singers, techies, internet creators, athletes and many others use their unique voice to attract great wealth.

A voice is not just the things you say, but it is a presence, and a special style that is all your own. Your Voice is akin to your fingerprint; it separates, and clarifies who you are. You came to this planet as an individual who brought with you unique talents and gifts. Your Gift of Voice tells the world you have arrived and that you have something valuable to say.

You have a great gift. The Gift of Voice sets you apart from every other human on the planet. Do not be afraid to use your voice. Never think what you have to say has no value. You came to this planet with something special inside you and the rest of the world cannot benefit from it if you keep what you have to say to yourself. Find ways to use it for your benefit. How can you use your Gift of Voice to attract wealth into your life?

_____

_____

_____

_____

_____

_____

_____

_____

_____

_____

_____

_____

_____

_____

_____

THE SEVENTH GIFT – THE GIFT OF LOVE

Remember Jack and his visit from The Powerful Ones? Do you remember the baby covered in the light of love? We must remember that each of us came to Earth full of love, and sometimes because of the hard-knocks of life that love is hard to see.

The greatest force in the world is Love. Sometimes it appears that evil people win but when you look back over history, Love has always won. People who have been trapped by other evil people have been set free by people who used Love to free them. When hate and violence kept people separated, non-violence and Love brought them together.

When the world around you feels the hardest and during those times life seems the darkest, you must look inside and find the Gift of Love. You must learn to look at all things through the eyes of Love. Never allow your heart to grow hard and callous, for if you do, the person harmed the most will be you. Instead, teach yourself to call upon your most special gift, the Gift of Love, and let Love direct your path.

The greatest force in the world is Love. By using Love you can overcome any obstacle. Love will help you understand difficult people and situations. How can you use the Gift of Love to respect and appreciate others?

_____

_____

_____

_____

_____

_____

_____

_____

_____

_____

_____

_____

_____

_____

The Gift of Love and Wealth

Age old wisdom says, "Do unto others as you would want others to do unto you." Everybody wants to be loved, whether they admit it or not. When you love yourself it is easy to love someone else. When you want great things to happen to others, it's easy for others to want great things to happen for you.

Sometimes people act hard because they have been treated hard. Do you know people like that? They have been hurt and that pain lives inside of them. Because they have been hurt so badly they hurt others.

When you meet people who are mean for no reason, you have to try to see the "Baby covered in Love." Don't try to meet them with the same anger and rage they bring to you, try to meet them with understanding and Love. Do not be fearful of them, instead be mindful of who they really are deep inside.

Selfishness is the #1 destroyer of Love. When we act selfishly we cut off Love. We must be careful not to think only of what we want. To be great, we have to consider the desires of others. As a young person, it is easy to think about you most of the time, because the adults in your life have always taken care of your needs. As you get older you have to look for ways where everybody wins.

Love equals trust. If someone shows you love over and over again you learn to trust them. When you show people you know how to love and do so over and over again, they will learn to trust you, too. The more people you treat lovingly the more your reputation will grow as a loving person. You will be amazed how many opportunities come your way, because you treat others with Love.

Love is energy and it can be felt by others. Love is not nervous, it is secure. When you enter a job interview and feel secure and loving, the person across from you can feel that presence. You do not have to do anything; just have the feeling on the inside. Your Love will make you feel comfortable and will help make the stranger you talk to comfortable as well.

Each of us can feel it when another person likes us. We can also feel it when a person is uncomfortable in our presence. People love to do business with people they like. When you send positive energy to each person you come in contact with you send the message you are likeable. How can the Gift of Love   help you attract wealth into your life?

_____

_____

_____

_____

_____

_____

_____

_____

Your Personal Road map!

Congratulations! You have just completed your personal road map. Your personal road map is your compass to power and greatness! By identifying your hidden gifts, you can now begin using them to accomplishing all of your goals and dreams.

Take some time and practice using your gifts. Learn how to use Awareness to be more aware of the things around you. Be proud of being Unique and one of a kind. Use the gift of Vision to see the life you want to live and then use your other gifts to bring that vision to life.

Learn to use the Gift of Creation, and start creating your new life. Be aware of the special things shown to you through your Imagination. You may discover something the world has been looking for. Find your Voice and learn to use it to direct your other great gifts. Fill your heart with Love and let Love direct your path. Give Love to others and watch that Love come back to you.

Put your road map (this book) somewhere close by, where you can read it often. Read it every day, until you can recite its every word. Let your road map become a part of you and you will grow in a mighty way. Before you go to bed, read a few pages of your roadmap, so you can think about your greatness, even when you sleep.

Jack was tricked into chasing money instead of seeking and developing his gifts. Everything he needed to be great was already inside him waiting to help him succeed.

It took Michael, his distant grandson to find out the secret of his hidden gifts, and use them to attract wealth, and restore Jack back home to the King. Don't allow yourself to be tricked into chasing money. Instead, look for your hidden treasures within, work hard on those natural talents, and those special gifts will make room for you in this world.

ONE PAGE GIFTS LIST

Awareness = What separates humans from animals? Humans can think and are aware we are thinking. The Gift of Awareness expands your world-view.

Vision = The ability to look beyond the present and see future possibilities.

Uniqueness = You are a one-of-a-kind MASTERPIECE! Be proud of your differences. You are just the way you are supposed to be.

Imagination = The realm where the future lives. Learn how to reach into your imagination and bring forth the treasures of tomorrow.

Creation = The ability to mold energy and things into something greater than they were.

Voice = The gift that tells the world you have arrived and have something valuable to say! Command all your other gifts with the powerful Gift of Voice .

Love = The greatest force on the planet. Your most precious gift. Your tool that enables you to connect with every human being on Earth. Love unites, calms, excites, expands, illuminates, attracts, binds, celebrates, empowers, and endures.

About The Author

WES HALL

Wes was blessed to have discovered his gifts and talents at an early age. At the age of 8 he was chosen for the lead role as the "Troll" in the play, "Billy Goats Gruff." He was voted Student Council President, of his 8th grade class and won a city-wide radio contest that required entrance's to write in 50 words or less why they should be the station's "Star DJ." That contest and his subsequent stint on the airwaves led Wes to a 20 year, on-air radio career. He has since broadcasted in some of the largest markets in the country including, Virginia, North Carolina, and Oakland/San Francisco.

In 1999 he wrote his debut book, "You Are the Money!" He revised the book and re-released it in 2007. After writing his book, Wes began a new career as a national motivational speaker. He attracted a top mentor by the name of Les Brown. Mr. Brown is a world-renowned speaker and best-selling author. Les and Wes share the same birthday and Les has a twin brother named Wes. Les taught Wes the ways of motivational speaking and the two have appeared on stage together.

Wes turned his sights to the field of education and used his gift of speaking and talent of training to help disadvantaged at-risk students understand the value of a good education. His efforts were so well received by the students that one school turned his program into an elective course and awarded a grade toward graduation to students who successfully completed the course.

His work was not complete, however, until he could find a way to deliver the message of "Self-Development equals Wealth-Development" to younger kids, and thus came, "Jack and the Sly Fox." This book represents 10 years of working with a concept and finally being able to condense it down to bites small enough for young people to digest.

Wes is proud to offer this book to any young person who desires to learn more about their natural gifts and talents and is prepared to do all it takes to develop them, and become the great person he/she is capable of becoming.

Wes currently resides in Los Angeles and is the host of the "You Are the Money – Self Investment radio show, on LA Talk Radio.

More information about Wes is available at:

http://connectioninitiative.blogspot.com/2013/01/ relationships-are-key-to-success.html

http://www.latalkradio.com/Hall.php

http://totallymotivated.blogspot.com/

Made in the USA
Middletown, DE
03 March 2022

62034153R00097